IN EVERY
MOON
THERE IS A FACE

This book is dedicated
to the Silence within us all
whose luminous Presence
within our own presence

shines

In Every Moon There Is a Face

Poem by Charles Mathes

Illustrations by Arlene Graston

ILLUMINATION Arts

PUBLISHING COMPANY, INC.

A TERRI COHLENE BOOK

This

is a story that words cannot tell,

so be sure to look and listen

with your heart.

In every Moon there is...

a *Face*

In every Face there is...

a T ree

And every Tree is full...

of *L*ace

And in that Lace you'll find...

a Sea

Above that Sea a cloud...

of **W***ords*

Hides underneath a quilt of Light
And in that light a crowd...

of **B***irds*

Becomes a small bright yellow Kite
And in that kite there is...

a *J*ar

That's full of Flowers growing wild
And in each flower there's...

a *Star*

And in each Star there is...

a *Child*

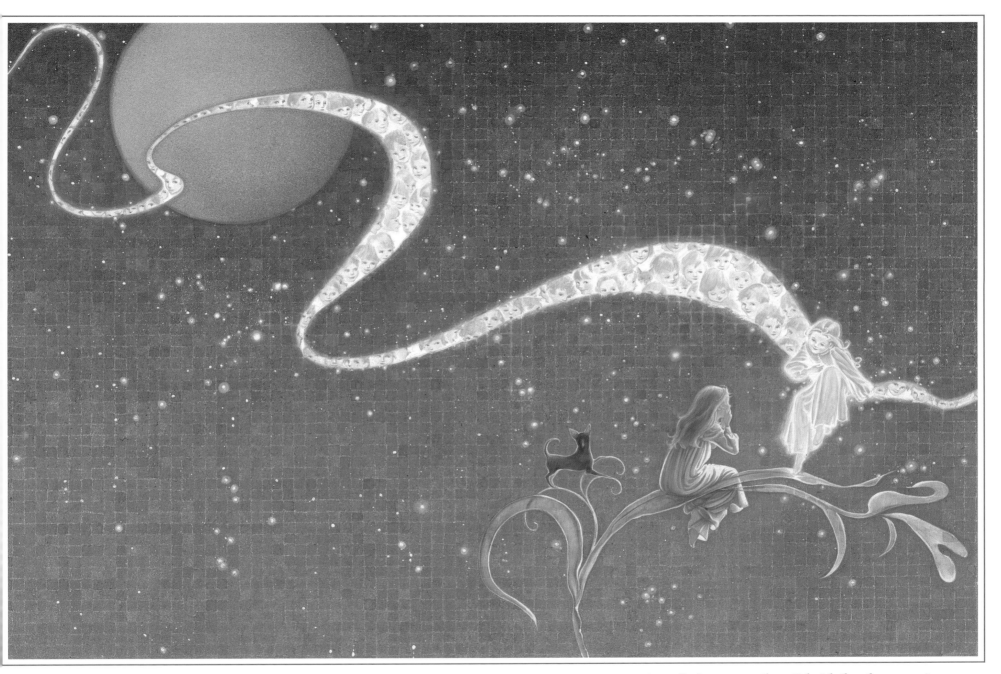

And in each Child there is...

a *Sky*

That's full of Daydreams and Balloons
And every dream's...

a Butterfly -

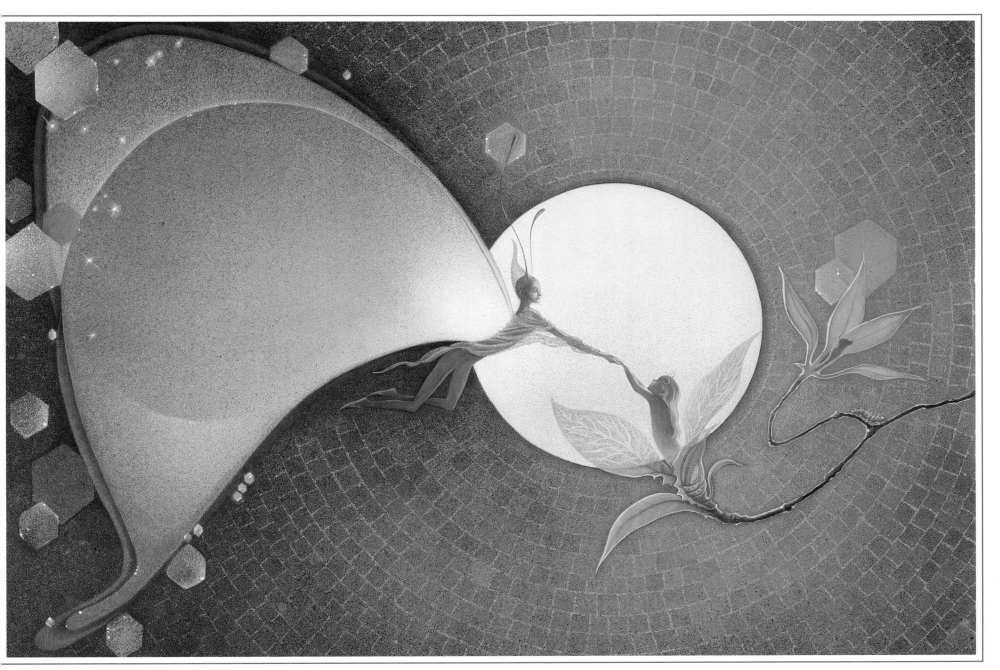

A Butterfly that's full...

of *M*oons

Text Copyright © 2003 by Charles Mathes • Illustrations Copyright © 2003 by Arlene Graston

Library of Congress Cataloging-in-Publication Data

Mathes, Charles.
    In every moon there is a face : poem / by Charles Mathes ; paintings by Arlene Graston.
        p. cm.
    Summary: A young girl takes a flight of fancy in which everything she sees leads her to
another image, such as a light which becomes a crowd of birds, which in turn becomes a kite.
    ISBN 0-9701907-4-3
    [1. Imagination—Fiction. 2. Stories in rhyme.] I. Graston, Arlene, ill. II. Title.

    PZ8.3.M4225 In 2003
    [E]—dc21
                                                                    200227514
Published in the United States of America

Photography and Pre-press by Gamma One Conversions, Inc., NYC
Printed by Star Standard Industries of Singapore • Book and Cover Design by Arlene Graston

ILLUMINATION

Arts

PUBLISHING COMPANY, INC.
P.O. BOX 1865
BELLEVUE, WA 98009

For a complete listing of our uplifting
children's books
contact us:
FAX: 425-644-9274
TEL: 425-644-7185 • 888-210-8216 (orders only)
liteinfo@illumin.com • www.illumin.com

ILLUMINATION ARTS PUBLISHING COMPANY, INC.
is a member of Publishers in Partnership – replanting our nation's forests.